11/17/10

THIS BOOK IS THE PROPERTY OF:

Issued To:	Condition	
	Issued	Returned
Fizban	**New**	Slightly burned (sorry, still getting hang of fireball.)
Taliesin	New	New (used repair spell)
Zendric	**New**	Spine broken by roommate, not my fault!
Raistlin Majere	teeth marks	Replaced Cover
Fordham the Tanner	**good**	Ale-stained—Sorry!
Xicara Craftmaker	Fair (pages wrinkled)	New (ironed pages, new cover made from dragon hide)
MALCHOR HARPELL	NEW	GOOD
RD Henham	good	good
Bob the Elf	Fair	More teeth marks, familiar likes chewing.

Pupils to whom this textbook is issued may write on any
page or mark any part in any way; spell-writing excepted.

Advice to Future Owners of This Book

Add your own suggestions below!

Ask an adult wizard before proceeding with any activities.

Don't use kitchen without permission from mentor.

All bottles should be enchanted glass (sometimes known as plaztick) to minimize breakage and injury.

NO!

Don't cut leaves or twigs off trees. Nymphs will come after you!.

Balloons used for holding garlic water shouldn't be too strong or they won't pop when thrown at a vampire.

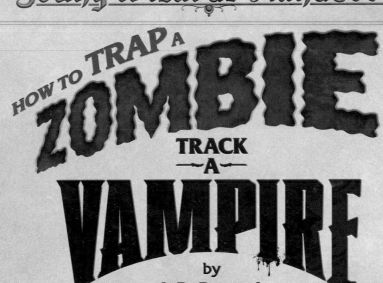

HOW TO TRAP A ZOMBIE
TRACK A VAMPIRE

by
A.R. Rotruck

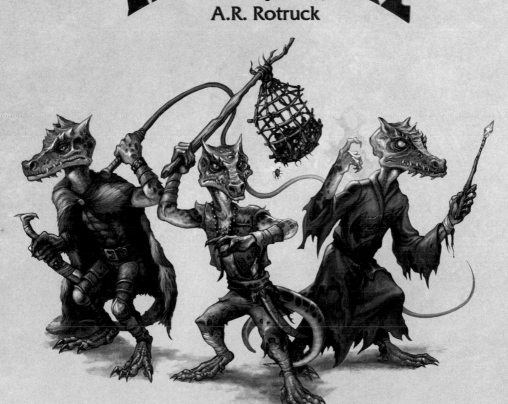

Wizards
OF THE COAST

BOOKS FOR
YOUNG READERS

Young Wizards Handbook:
How to Trap a Zombie, Track a Vampire, and Other Hands-On Activities for Monster Hunters

Cover Art by Wayne England

Interior Art by Miguel Coimbra, Tony DiTerlizzi, Wayne England, Emily Fiegenschuh,
Carl Frank, Lars Grant-West, Ralph Horsley, Doug Kovacs, Howard Lyon, Beth Trott, Jim Nelson,
William O'Connor, Lucio Parrillo, Steve Prescott, Ron Spears, Anne Stokes, Franz Vohwinkel,
Eva Widermann, Sam Wood, James Zhang, UDON

Art Direction by Kate Irwin
Graphic Design by Jino Choi

First Printing: September 2010

Library of Congress Cataloging-in-Publication Data

Rotruck, A.R.
  Young wizards handbook : how to trap a zombie, track a vampire, and other hands-on activities for monster hunters / by A.R. Rotruck.
    p. cm.
  ISBN 978-0-7869-5548-0
  1. Monsters--Juvenile literature. 2. Hunting--Juvenile literature. 3. Survival skills--Juvenile literature. I. Title.
  GR825.R68 2010
  398'.469--dc22

                                                              2010010868

9 8 7 6 5 4 3 2 1
ISBN: 978-0-7869-5548-0
620-183690000-001-EN

U.S., CANADA,
ASIA, PACIFIC, & LATIN AMERICA
Wizards of the Coast LLC
P.O. Box 707
Renton, WA 98057-0707
+1-800-324-6496

EUROPEAN HEADQUARTERS
Hasbro UK Ltd
Caswell Way
Newport, Gwent NP9 0YH
GREAT BRITAIN
Please keep this address for your records

dungeonsanddragons.com

For Brian, my partner
in monster hunting and
everything else. Thank you for
all the recipe help, wilderness
survival tips, support, and of
course, love!

Contents

INTRODUCTION

While there are many paths a young wizard might take, there are none so exciting and rewarding as that of a monster-hunting wizard. Solving riddles posed by sphinxes, rescuing towns from goblin packs, or recovering treasure from an ogre are just some of the fascinating tasks a monster-hunting wizard may be asked to do.

How to Evaluate Danger

When hunting monsters, remember, looks can be deceiving! Not all monsters look particularly dangerous: some may appear non-threatening, comical, or even downright cute. Also bear in mind that many monsters practice illusion. But magical illusions cannot trick an observant young wizard.

You do not neccesarily have to cast a spell to penetrate illusion and evaluate the threat of an approaching monster. Just use your senses. The core rules for any monster hunter boil down to the three Ss: Sight, Smell, and Sound.

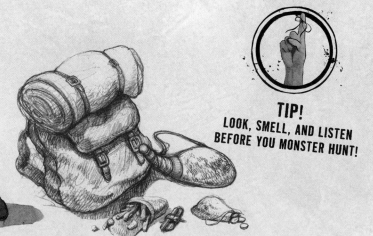

TIP!
LOOK, SMELL, AND LISTEN
BEFORE YOU MONSTER HUNT!

Sight[1]

This may not come naturally to wizards used to reading spellbooks. But when you embark on a monster hunt, you must watch for everything! Sight is associated with the color blue and the element of water, which is sometimes clear, sometimes murky.

Smell

Monsters and other animals have distinctive smells. Legend tells of one wizard who could pinpoint the age of a vampire from a hundred feet away! Spell components have particular scents as well. If the monster has magical powers, the odors around it can serve as a clue. Follow your nose; it can keep you safe! Smell is associated with the color green and the element of earth, which provides such a rich variety of odors.

Sound

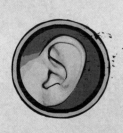

Surely your teachers have told you to listen, and they're absolutely right! Sight needs help. That's why you need to remember to listen to everything. What happens at night? What if you have a blindness spell cast on you? That is why any enchanted music-listening objects that go directly in the ear should be left at home when monster hunting. Sound is associated with the color yellow and the element of air, which carries sound to all ears.

---

1 You'll notice that only three of the five basic senses are listed here. That is because when dealing with monsters and other dangers, you should avoid tasting and touching whenever possible!

GATHERING SUPPLIES

A monster hunting wizard needs many supplies. From the tools to trap or trick monsters to the gear you need to survive, the items on these pages are essential to any monster-hunting quest.

How to Make a Monster-Hunting Pack[2]

Before you go on any monster hunting adventure, you'll need a special bag to hold your supplies. You can make one of your own out of an old pair of pants.

- One old pair of pants
- Scissors
- Needle

- Thread
- Two pieces of cord, two feet long

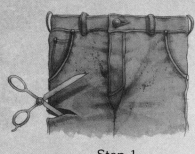

Step 1

Step 2

Steps 3–4

Steps 5–6

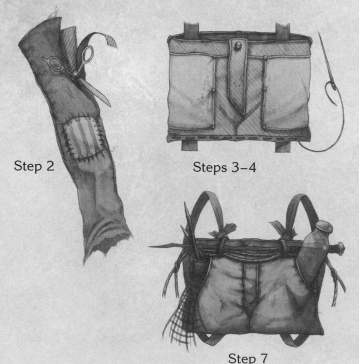

Step 7

---

[2] Also known as Heward's Handy Haversack, after Heward the Handy.

1) Cut the legs off. Be careful not to cut through the pocket lining.

2) Cut out two long strips, each about 3 inches wide, from one of the legs. These will be the straps for the pack.

3) Turn pants inside out.

4) Place the straps on the inside of the leg holes, lining the edge of each strap with the edge of each leg hole. Stitch the leg holes closed, sewing the bottom edge of the straps to the bag.

5) Turn the pants right-side-out and tie the top of each strap to a belt loop.[3]

6) String one piece of cord through the belt loops so the loose ends open at the right side of the bag. Tie the ends. Repeat with the loose ends opening at the left side of the bag.

7) Pull cords tight. Your pack is done!

---

[3] You may need to re-tie straps to get a good fit for your pack.

[4] You may wish to add more items depending on what kind of monsters you plan to hunt.

[5] Lest you follow in the footsteps of Clothilde the Clumsy, whose pack exploded when she tripped and broke all her glass bottles of liquid potions, then disappeared in a poof of spellsmoke.

[6] All clothing should be double-duty if possible. Enchanted boots, cloaks, and even underwear all save magic energy and keep you warm and safe.

Monster Hunting Gear

Before embarking on any adventure, at the very least you will need the following items:[4]

- Unbreakable[5] bottles with essential potions and drinking water
- Food (dried fruit or meat)
- Clothing[6]
- Monster catcher (see page 16)
- Staff and/or wand components (see page 15)
- Cards, marbles, or other small games
- Several sheets of blank, gridded paper stored in your scroll case (see page 20)
- Pencil
- A belt with pouches for carrying extra supplies
- Wax and/or cotton for earplugs
- This book

Do not bring any valuables with you unless they are enchanted. It attracts unnecessary attention from robbers and dragons, so unless it will aid you magically, leave it at home! If you must bring it, tuck it out of sight.

How to Find the Right Staff

Some wizards claim that a staff should be the fourth "S" of the monster-hunting wizard. A staff has many practical functions such as walking stick, weapon, and even tent pole. It can be thin or thick, long or short, heavy oak or lightweight bamboo. Whatever you choose, it must fit your hand and your temperament. Otherwise, any magic you attempt while using the staff will fail or, worse, go awry! Cutting a staff from a living tree rather than finding one on the ground can also cause unexpected and undesirable magic.

Don't underestimate a staff that has only simple magical features, such as creating light or generating one meal a day. Sure, everyone wants a staff that can deal a stunning blow to a giant. But the odds of running into a giant are far less than the odds of running short of food.

Before setting off on any adventures, walk around for a day carrying and using your staff to make sure it won't feel too heavy or give you splinters.

TIP!
CHOOSE A STAFF
THAT CAN DOUBLE AS
A WALKING STICK.

Wood	Personality Trait	Good for:
Oak	Resourceful	Defense
Maple	Intelligent	Detection
Pine	Caring	Healing
Bamboo	Light-hearted	Illusion
Aspen	Artistic	Levitation
Dogwood	Loyal	Protection
Willow	Wise	Knowledge

Color	Traditional Meaning	Aids Magic for:
Red	Determination	Fire-related spells (fire)
Yellow	Hope	Basic survival (warmth, meal generation)
Orange	Bounty	Earth-related spells
Green	Growth	Magic related to plants or animals (speak with animals)
Blue	Contemplation	Water-related spells (underwater breathing, water purification)
Purple	Creativity	Illusion, change form
White	Helpfulness	Feather fall
Black	Focus	Basic enchantments
Brown	Resourcefulness	Changing materials (enlargement, thin metal)
Gold	Protection	Shielding
Silver	Imagination	Trickery (ghost sounds, illusion)
Iridescent	Wisdom	Information (detect magic)

Staff Adornments

Even if you have an inexpensive, generic staff, you can both make your spellcasting stronger and personalize your staff by adorning it with colorful items. Use the color chart above as a guide.

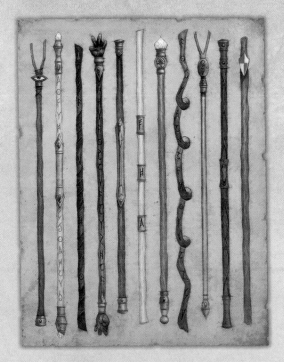

13

How to Improvise a Wand

While most monster-hunting wizards prefer a staff to focus their magic, some choose wands because they are more portable and easier to conceal. Best of all, if something happens to your wand in the midst of a monster battle, you can easily improvise a new one.

To make a wand, look around for tree branches lying on the ground. Do NOT cut the branch from the tree! Refer to the wood chart on page 12 to determine which type of wood best suits your spellcasting needs. Write or paint your initials or insignia on the wand. This quickens the bond between you and the wand. Tie or glue various wand components such as seeds, leaves, small stones, or feathers to the wand. Use the chart at right as a guide.

Wand Components

Adding components to your wand can bend your wand toward the type of magic you require. Many of these components you can find at a moment's notice.

Wand Component	Where to Find	Use
Acorn cap	Beneath oak tree	Enlargement spells
Cactus needle	Beneath cactus	Defensive spells
Cat's claw	Your familiar (Ask if you can cut her claws. Be careful!)	Offensive spells
Four-leaf clover	In an open field	Improves aim
Griffon fur	On bushes where the griffon scratches its neck	Flight spells
Holly leaf	On holly tree	Daze spell
Lace	Your family's sewing basket	Aids illusion
Lizard scale	On ground in desert	Silence spells
Mermaid hair	A friendly mermaid (Ask first!)	Water spells
Metal bits	Anywhere	Alarm spells
Mushroom spores	Dried mushrooms	Sleep spells
Phoenix feather	Dropped by a phoenix upon a worthy wizard	Fire spells
Rose petal	Rose when it is fully open	Love or friendship spells (Use cautiously!)
Snake skin	On ground after snake sheds	Change spells
Snowflake	In winter sky (catch ten on your wand)	Weather spells
Unicorn tail hair	Unicorn (Must be given freely!)	Shield spells

Before you leave on a monster hunt, examine your wand for cracks or splinters, and check that all decoration and magical components are firmly attached. The belt loops in your monster-hunting pack are a convenient place to store your wand. You can also hide your wand up your sleeve, tuck it into your belt, or stuff it down a high boot.

How to Make a Monster Catcher

A monster-catching net is one of the most essential tools for the adventuring wizard. With the right items tied into the string, this net can immobilize or at least slow down any creature imaginable. You can use a simple enlargement spell once you know how big the monster is, so you only need a small net in your monster-hunting kit.

- Ball of string or yarn
- Materials for tie-ins (see list)
- One chair with four legs

1) Tip a chair on its side so the legs are pointing at you.

2) Tie a length of string between the top two chair legs to form a line.[7]

3) Cut ten strings twice as long as the distance between the chair legs. Fold each string in half.

4) Place the fold of one string over the string between the chair legs. Pull the loose ends through the fold, forming a knot around the line.[8]

5) Repeat with each folded string until you have tied all ten strings to the chair string. Space out the strings evenly.

6) Take the right string of the first string pair and tie it to the left string of the second string pair, using an overhand knot. This will form a triangle shape. Repeat with each string pair until you have created a row of triangles.

7) Return to the first string pair. Tie the two far left strings together, using an overhand knot.

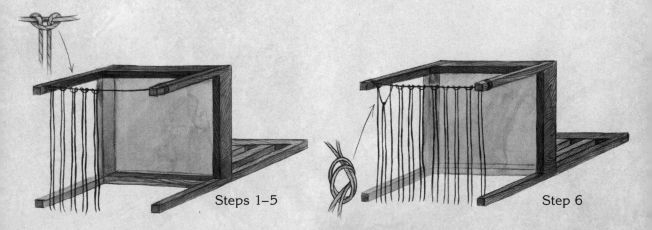

Steps 1–5

Step 6

---

7 The strings in steps 2 and 10 should be VERY tight lines!
8 This type of knot is called a lark's head.

8) Tie the right string from the first triangle to the left string of the next triangle. Now you have a diamond shape. Repeat until you have a row of diamonds.

9) Repeat steps 6–8 until you are left with an inch of string.

10) Tie a string to the bottom two chair legs to form another horizontal line.

11) Tie loose ends from the last row of diamonds to the bottom line. Trim ends.

12) Tuck materials related to the creature you're hunting into the net (see chart below). You can either make lots of nets, each for a different creature. Or if you're pressed for time or have very little room in your monster-hunting bag, tie a sample of each material into the net.

13) Untie or cut string from chair legs and remove net. When you're ready to use the net, cast an enlargement spell.

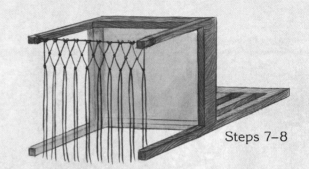

Steps 7–8

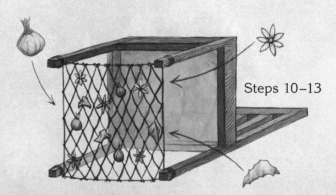

Steps 10–13

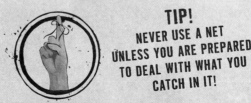

TIP!
NEVER USE A NET UNLESS YOU ARE PREPARED TO DEAL WITH WHAT YOU CATCH IN IT!

Monster	Material Needed
Werewolf	Bits of silver (if shiny, also can be used for medusa)
Vampire	Cloves of garlic
Medusa	Small reflective pieces of metal or thin metal (see page 54)
Goblin	Small coins or jewels
Kraken	Seaweed
Beholder	Daisies or other flowers that look like eyes
Ghost	Salt water (soak net in salt water for three minutes)

How to Make Travel Garb

A wizard needs two main clothing items when traveling on an adventure: short robes and a cloak. If you cannot purchase these at your local wizarding shop, make your own!

Short Robes

- One old pillowcase
- Scissors
- Ribbon, cord, or belt
- Decorative pens or paints

1) Hold the pillowcase open end down.

2) Cut a half-moon shape in the middle of the closed end of the pillowcase. It should be no more than a foot wide, just enough to put your head through. You can widen if needed.

3) Leaving about two inches from the top of the pillowcase, cut another half-moon shape on the side seam, no more than six inches long. If you cut small, you can always make it bigger.

4) Repeat step 3 for the other side of the pillowcase.

5) Pull the pillowcase over your head and belt it with ribbon, cord, or a belt. The robe can be worn with pants and shoes or boots.

6) Decorate your robe any way you'd like. Keep in mind that muted colors are much better for passing unnoticed while exploring. Grays, browns, tans, and muted greens will help you blend into the natural surroundings.

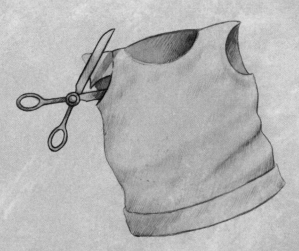

Cloak

- One old blanket
- Ribbon about two feet long
- Needle and thread

1) Fold top seam of blanket over so you have about a one-inch pocket at the top.

2) Stitch along bottom side of the pocket. Be sure to leave both ends of the pocket open.

3) Run a ribbon, cord, or string through the pocket.

4) Tie the ribbon around your neck and drape the blanket down around your shoulders.

5) Have a friend make a mark on the blanket just above the tops of your shoes.

6) Cut the blanket level with the mark. You can always cut it shorter if you like.[9]

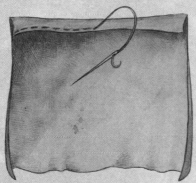

Steps 1–2

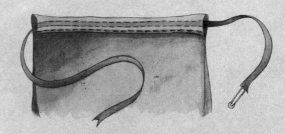

Step 3

Steps 4–6

TIP!
TIE A KNOT IN THE RIBBON SO YOU CAN PUSH IT EASILY THROUGH THE POCKET, OR USE A METAL CLOAK PIN.

---

[9] Keep the extra strip of blanket. You can use it as a belt for your robe.

How to Make a Scroll Case

As a monster hunter, you will need to carry lots of papers: maps, complicated spell instructions, notes on various monsters, gridded paper for mapping new dungeons, and plain paper for making enchanted vessels (see page 61) and for impromptu monster games. Be sure to bring this scroll case to make sure your papers stay safe and crinkle-free!

- One tube[10]
- Strips of fabric or rope for carrying strap
- Large needle
- Piece of string or yarn six inches long
- Two pieces of cork or other thick, lightweight material about one inch thick[11]
- Glue
- Ink or paint

1) Cut two circular pieces of cork or similar material to fit inside each end of the tube.

2) Glue one of the pieces of cork to the end of the tube.

3) Knot the string at one end. Using the needle, poke a hole through the other piece of cork and draw the string through it.

4) Now poke a hole in the tube with the needle about a half inch from the open end.

5) Pull the string into the tube through the hole. Remove the needle. Then knot the end of the string so that it can't be pulled out of the hole.

6) Insert the cork in the open end of the tube. Now you have a removable cap to use for your scroll case.

---

10 Towels or paper purchased at the village shop come rolled on tubes about a foot in length. These tubes are ideal for storing most maps and scrolls.

11 There is a mysterious substance, found only in very special lands, that is even lighter and easier to manipulate than cork. Such a substance is often white and is called floom or foam or something of that sort. Should you come across this material, you are a very lucky wizard indeed!

7) Tie and glue the carrying strap to the tube. You can either glue a long strap to both ends and carry the case across your back, or glue a smaller strap to one end and tie it to your belt. If you don't want a strap, you can always place the case in your monster-hunting pack.

8) Decorate your scroll case with ink or paint.

TIP!
YOU CAN USE THE EXTRA STRIPS FROM YOUR ADVENTURING BAG OR CLOAK FOR A CARRYING STRAP.

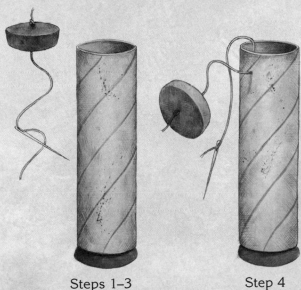

Steps 1–3

Step 4

Step 5

Steps 6–8

How to Concoct Essential Potions

Brew up a batch of each one of these easy-to-make potions, before you head out on your monster hunt.

Revitalizing Draught

This beverage is delicious and easy to make. It also travels well. Just remember to shake before drinking if it's been sitting in your flask a while.

- One large clear jar with lid
- Three tea bags

1) Fill jar with water.

2) Add tea bags.

3) Close jar and set in a sunny place. (A windowsill is perfect.)

4) Let sit for three hours. Return and witness the magical transformation of your draught.

5) On hot days, or when hunting sphinxes in the desert, drink the draught over ice.

6) On cool days, or when hunting yetis in the frozen tundra, ask an adult wizard to heat the draught for you. Enjoy in a mug with some honey.

Invisible Ink

If you want to send a secret message to another wizard, invisible ink is an absolute must!

- ¼ cup lemon juice
- 1 tablespoon salt
- Fine paintbrush
- Paper
- Wax crayon or light source

TIP!
THIS RECIPE TRAVELS WELL IN A FLASK.

1) Using lemon juice and a fine paintbrush, write your message on paper.

2) Sprinkle salt on the juice while it's still wet.

3) Let dry. (Overnight is best.)

4) Once dry, wipe the salt off.

5) The person who receives the message may read it in two ways: by rubbing a wax crayon on the paper or by holding it up to a hot light source.[12]

---

[12] Be careful not to set the paper afire lest you lose the message.

Tanglefoot Potion

This mysterious potion can't decide if it's a liquid or solid, which makes it very easy to trap things in it . . . including yourself!

- 1 cup corn starch
- ½ cup water
- Red and green food coloring (optional)
- Bowl
- Clear, flexible bags

1) Pour water in bowl.

2) If this is for a zombie trap, adding one drop each of red food coloring and one drop green to the water will color the finished mixture brown. For a browner shade, add another drop red. For a grayer shade, add another drop green. Keep the surrounding area in mind when creating color.

3) Add corn starch about a spoonful at a time, mixing constantly.

4) Once all the corn starch is added, keep mixing. It may take a while and it gets tough, so take turns with a friend. When it becomes too tough to stir with a spoon, your hands work best.

5) Potion is done when it looks liquid, but if you move your hands through it, it feels more solid. You should be able to pick some of it up in your hands and, when squeezed, see some of the dry corn starch.

6) If your potion is too liquid, add more corn starch a tablespoon at a time. If too solid, add more water a tablespoon at a time.

7) Place in a bag for future use. If you need to keep your laboratory neat, try mixing the potion directly in the bag. The bag should not leak while you carry it, but should be able to burst open upon impact. Unless circumstances are dire, use only outside!

SURVIVING Your SURROUNDINGS

Often the greatest danger isn't the monsters you hunt, but the land itself. It isn't enough to know how to survive a monster attack. You must know how to survive your surroundings too.

How to Survive a Monster-Hunting Quest

The major dangers in the wilderness are:

- Disorientation
- Hunger
- Cold
- Injury

All of these dangers are very real and very serious. To the well-prepared wizard, though, they can be but minor annoyances. Always mark your trail with signs that do not disturb the environment (such as piles of rocks, see page 44) to ensure you won't get lost. If you travel with enough food and know the local flora, you should never go hungry. By traveling with warm clothes, a bedroll, and simple shelter, you can weather all but the most frigid storms. For injury, study how to treat simple wounds.[13] Also, you should always keep at least one companion with you, if not more. (See page 26.)

Above all else, always travel with plenty of water. While water is heavy, it is the most important survival tool you can bring. While there are water-purifying spells and magical tablets, you cannot always be assured of finding water at all, let alone water suitable for drinking. Bring a few flasks, canteens, or unbreakable bottles on every monster-hunting trip.

---

[13] Healing is far too complicated a magic to be covered in this text. Refer to other magical and medical texts, such as R.D. Henham's *Chomped! Complete Guide to Field-Dressing Dragon Bites*. Better yet, take the "Magical Mending" class; it's offered at most wizardry schools.

How to Form a Monster-Hunting Party

While the idea of being a lone monster hunter does seem exciting, in reality monster hunting is best undertaken with a party of fellow hunters. Many wands make light work, as the old saying goes.

When putting together a monster-hunting party, consider all ages and types of personalities, not just your friends! Often you need people who think differently to ensure that the group can imagine all possibilities. An elven ranger is going to have a very different outlook than a dwarf fighter. Never discount anyone who might have a key skill or a talent for fighting monsters!

The basic roles you should have in your monster party fall into four categories: controller, defender, leader, and striker. It's best to invite one from each category if possible.

If you have more than four people who want to join your party, that's fine. You can always use a few extra defenders or strikers. If you have fewer than four people, that's fine too. It just means that everyone in your group will have to work a little bit harder to keep the group safe from monster attacks.

TIP!
MAKE SURE EVERY
MEMBER OF YOUR PARTY
HAS A COPY OF THIS BOOK.

Controllers

Controllers are usually wizards (which, if you're reading this book, likely means you!). They tend to strategize and organize. They are the thinkers of the group. A good thinker, though, always remembers to listen to other people's ideas.

Defenders

Defenders are most often basic fighters (knights, warriors, and mercenaries). They're usually the muscle of the group, but don't underestimate their common-sense approach.

Leaders

Leaders are typically clerics or warlords who help to protect and motivate your party. Clerics are dedicated servants of religion who can both fight and heal. Warlords are more advanced fighters who have good combat skills and are also skilled at motivating people.

Strikers

Strikers such as a rangers, rogues, or warlocks, are always ready to step up and take on a monster with a striking blow. They are the most acrobatic of the group, tumbling and moving around enemies with ease. They also tend to be clever at tricking monsters and disabling traps.

How to Secure Your Position

When monster hunting, you will spend many nights outdoors. It's important to choose a safe location so you won't awake to a gang of goblins or a pack of werewolves surrounding you!

Start looking for a place to spend the night when the sun first begins to set. Choose a location with cover, like a grove of trees or a cave. Scout the area to see if there are any signs of monsters nearby. The last place you want to camp is in a goblin's lair!

Once you've chosen a location, you may need to build or improve upon an already existing shelter. When building a shelter, do not take branches from trees with dryads and take care not to disturb the environment more than you must.

How to Construct a Shelter

Before you build your shelter, determine what direction the strongest wind is blowing. Then set up the shelter so it protects you from that wind.

- One blanket or cloak
- Ball of twine or heavy string
- Two pegs or sticks at least three inches long

1) Tie string between two trees or other sturdy structures using an overhand knot (see page 16). Height should be just above your head when you are seated.

2) Cut four one-foot lengths of string. Tie each length to a corner of the blanket using a lark's head knot (see page 16).

3) Tie two corners of blanket to line between trees, using an overhand knot.

4) Insert two pegs or sticks into the ground. Tie the other two corners of blanket to the pegs or sticks.

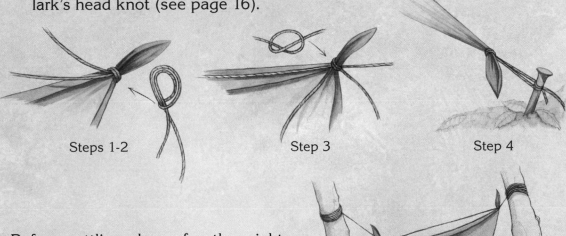

Steps 1-2   Step 3   Step 4

Before settling down for the night, cover your tracks and use brush to conceal your campsite. If you're lucky enough to find a cave, hide the entrance with brush and debris.

No matter how secure you make your location, someone or something should ALWAYS be on guard. If you're adventuring with friends, take turns being on watch. If you're on your own, cast a watchdog or alarm spell.

How to Find Food

By midday on your first hunt, your stomach will sound like a zombie underwater. That is why you packed plenty of nuts, dried fruit, and dried meat in your bag. But, if you run out of food and you happen to be in a land filled with edible plants, take a look around you and see if you might find something to sustain you.

While the lands where one might hunt monsters vary far too much to provide a complete guide, here are some of the more common edible plants that require little or no preparation. Before eating any local plant, be sure to identify it using a guide to your local flora and ask an adult wizard for permission to eat it. The elves offer a few courses of study on what one can eat in the wild and how best to prepare it. If you have an elf in your party, he or she can help as well.

- Bushes—strawberries, raspberries, blackberries

- Trees—apples, peaches, pears, oranges

- Other—mint leaves, sunflower seeds, wild onions, pumpkins, squash, honeysuckle

Avoid eating these!

TIP!
NEVER, EVER
EAT ANY KIND OF LOCAL
BERRY, FRUIT, OR PLANT
WITHOUT FIRST CHECKING
WITH AN ADULT WIZARD.

Never eat something unless you are certain it is edible. Mushrooms, for example, are so hard to identify that they're best left alone. Some kinds of berries are very colorful and look delicious, but are very poisonous.

In addition to plants that can kill you when you bite into them, there are also plants that will bite you! Avoid not just the giant flytraps who can snap you up in a single bite, but also vines that snake around unsuspecting ankles, trapping their victim for later consumption.

When you do find edible fruits, you can preserve them so they will travel well. You can do this either at home before you leave or perhaps an inn you stop at during your travels will allow you to use the oven.

How to Preserve Fruit for Travel

- 1 cup fruit (berries or apples work best)
- 2 tablespoons honey
- Metal tray or cookie sheet
- Wax paper
- Oven

1) Blend fruit and honey until smooth. If using berries, this won't take long. Harder fruits like apples need to be puréed.

2) Cover tray with wax paper.

3) Spread mixture into a thin layer on waxed paper.

4) Cook for three hours (or more) at 130 degrees. Mixture is done when fruit is dry; check at fifteen-minute intervals after three hours.

5) Remove from oven and let cool.

6) Once cooled, peel off tray.

7) Cut the dried fruit into strips and roll up for best travel.

How to Stay Warm without Fire

While fire provides warmth and comfort on the hunt, it attracts monsters and reveals your position to other humans, a definite no-no when deep in enemy territory. Add the always-present danger of a fire getting out of hand, and fire just isn't worth the danger or effort.

The good news is that fires really aren't necessary when hunting. With some planning, you can stay warm in all but the coldest weather—fire-free.

Bedroll

You've already learned how to make a shelter (on page 29). A shelter can protect you from both wind and water, two elements that can suck the warmth from you like a lich drains life. Once you're ready to go to sleep, a bedroll can keep you warm and toasty all night long.

- One heavy blanket or fur hide that resists water[14]
- Three regular blankets
- One sheet

---

[14] Some wizards have found that the "plaztick" spell can create an entirely waterproof blanket or tarp. Worth looking for at your local wizarding supply shop!

1) Lay the heavy blanket or fur hide on the ground.

2) Lay the first blanket on top of the heavy blanket so the edge of the first blanket is lined up with the center of the heavy blanket underneath.

3) Lay the second blanket on top of the first, lined up with the center of the first blanket. (In other words, it will be centered over the heavy blanket.)

4) Lay the third blanket on top of the second so it is centered over the first blanket.

5) Lay the sheet on top of third blanket so it's centered over the second blanket and heavy blanket.

6) Starting with sheet, fold each layer in half. You can put clothing or flat equipment on top of any layer before folding.

7) Once it is all folded, roll the bed roll. (Hence the name!)

8) Tie with rope. You can either carry on your back or slung across your shoulder.

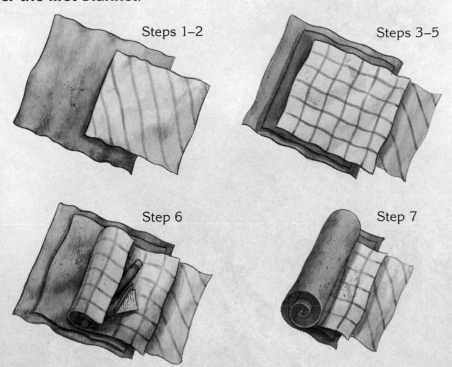

Steps 1–2   Steps 3–5

Step 6   Step 7

If your bedroll isn't quite warm or soft enough, put more layers between it and the ground. These layers can be dried moss, fallen leaves, pine needles (non-sticky ones!), or other old blankets.

How to Survive a Battle

There comes a time in every adventuring wizard's life when he or she ends up in the middle of a battle. If you're in a battle, the absolutely worst place is the front lines. There you run the risk of getting arrows or spells sent at you from both sides, not just one. You should stay near the rear of the fighting or, if possible, up a tree or on a cliff. That not only takes you out of the melee, it gives you a better line of sight for casting spells.

Remember, not all spells have to cause actual physical damage! Use sleep spells, blindness spells, or deafness spells, and any spell that just causes confusion. However, take careful aim so the magic does not affect your friends and allies. (And never forget which spells affect everyone in range!)

How to Fight with Slime

Slime is a good all-purpose way to distract your enemies in a battle. Some humans and even monsters are disgusted by slime and will run away when pelted with it. Those who aren't disgusted by slime are fascinated by it and will begin poking and playing with it and might very well forget about you!

- 1 cup (8 oz) glue
- 1½ cups warm water
- 1 tablespoon borax
- Food coloring
- Two bowls
- Bag

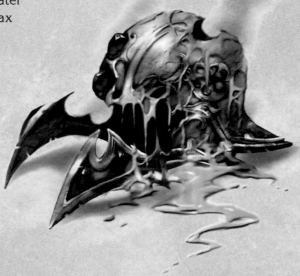

1) In one bowl, combine glue, 1 cup warm water, and a few drops of food coloring. Let cool to room temperature.

2) In the other bowl, combine the borax and ½ cup water.

3) Slowly add the glue mixture to the borax mixture. Stir until mixture becomes cohesive and feels rubbery.

4) Either use now or place in bag for transportation.[15]

---

[15] You can prepare part of slime ahead of time. Simply fill one flask with the white glue and water mixture, another with the borax and water solution. When ready to make slime, shake both flasks, pour all of glue and water mixture into a waterproof bag, add the borax mixture, shake the bag, and ta-da! Instant slime!

How to Navigate a Dungeon

Well, it was bound to happen. During your monster hunting you took a wrong turn and somehow ended up lost in a dungeon or series of caves so complicated it's a maze. It happens. While your situation may look hopeless, with a little observation and creative thinking, you can escape.

Even though it's hard to stay cheery when you're lost, try not to be discouraged and instead pay attention to everything around you. Don't forget to use all of your senses. Feel for air rushing by you. This could be a sign of an exit nearby. Listen to see if you can hear anyone. You never know, your companions might just be on the other side of the wall. Remember every detail. It could help later!

TIP!
MEMORIZE A TALK TO ANIMALS SPELL SO YOU CAN COMMUNICATE WITH RATS. THEY MIGHT SHOW YOU THE EXIT IN EXCHANGE FOR SOME FOOD.

As you search for the exit, use thread or make small marks on the walls to indicate where you are and where you went. If you reach an intersection, draw an arrow pointing which way you went, so if you find yourself there again, you can keep track of every turn you've made. You may also want to make a map to track your progress (see page 42), using the gridded paper you've stored in your scroll case.

Practice navigating the dungeon at right. Start at the skulls at top. Can you grab the sword, the shield, and the crown, and exit at the bottom right, by touching less than 30 squares?

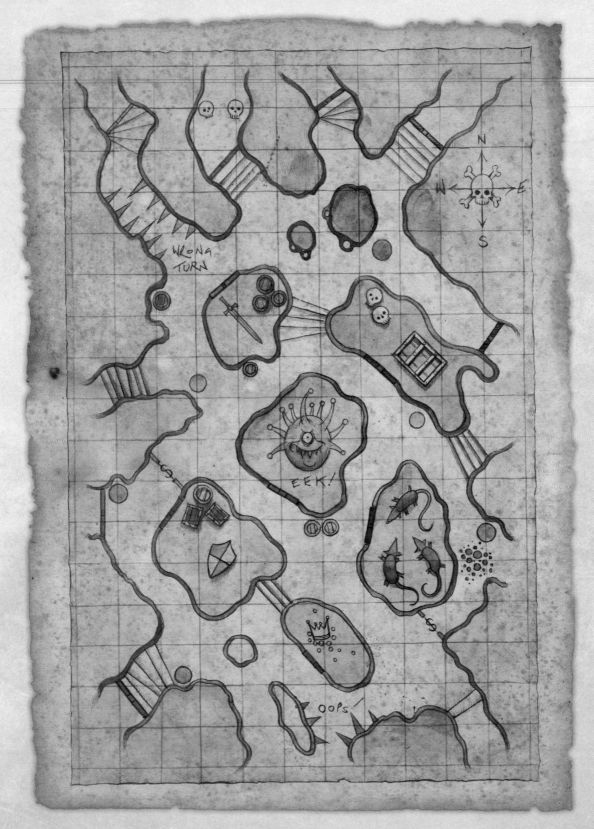

How to Make a Lantern

While some wizards are lucky enough to have a staff or wand to produce light, any light spells drain magical power which you may wish to save for your monster-hunting efforts. You can light your way without sapping your magical strength with sunrods or a lantern. If you can't afford to buy any of these items, it's easy to make a lantern on your own.

- One cardboard container such as those used for storing oats
- One magical light[16] and power source[17]
- Pipe cleaners
- Thin metal (see page 55 for details)
- Modeling clay
- Glue

1) Cover inside of container with thin metal, using glue if needed to keep it in place.

2) Cut small windows in container. This could look like a grid of squares or lots of random holes like Swiss cheese. A good design is pictured right. Remember, the more holes, the more light you will have.

3) Paint the container any color you like, although a color that will blend into surroundings, such as brown or gray, is the preferred design.

4) Roll clay into a lump and set on the bottom of the container.

---

[16] In some lands, these are called "flashlights" or "torches."
[17] Gnomes have developed power sources that they call "batteries."

5) Set magical light in clay so it won't roll around.

6) If desired, cut a small hole or door near the light switch so you can reach it without opening the lantern.

7) Poke two small holes directly opposite each other about one inch from the top of the container.

8) Thread pipe cleaner through the holes.[18]

9) Replace top.

10) Twist ends of pipe cleaner together, forming a hanger.

11) When hunting or camping, hang the lantern from a tree or rock outcropping.

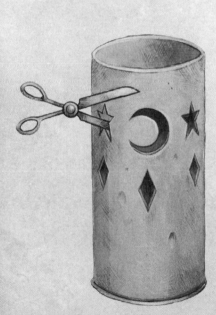

Steps 1–3

Steps 4–8

Steps 9–10

---

18 You can make a longer hanger by twisting more pipe cleaners together.

How to Check for Traps

As if adventuring wasn't dangerous enough, some villains and monsters place traps. Traps, unfortunately, can be anywhere: indoors, outdoors, floor, ceiling, even under and over water. They can also be anything: animate, inanimate, magical, mundane.

While the exact execution of traps may vary, they all have two basic parts—a trigger and the trap itself. A trap is worthless if it won't spring when needed. You can spot a trap by looking for either the trigger or the trap itself. If you can figure out the trigger, you just need to know how to avoid it. If you can see the trap, you just need to know how to get out of the way in time. Look for items that don't belong or seem odd in some way. Remember the three Ss!

Sights

Are there:
- Cracks roughly the size and shape of a doorway?
- Objects of immense value lying around?
- Taut strings, especially nearly invisible ones?

Smells

Are there:
- Spell component odors (pine, sulfur, lemon, wet dog)?
- Animal or monster smells?
- Smells that don't belong?

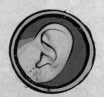

Sounds

Are there:
- Mechanical clicks?
- Grunting or growls from an unseen monster?
- Faint breezes or puffs of air?[19]

[19] Use fine dust thrown in the air to confirm breezes or drafts.

When checking for traps, divide the area into a grid, either mentally or on paper. Examine and search each square of the grid before setting foot onto it. Once you've established that square is safe, move on to the next.

Trap Game

You can practice searching for traps with a friend. Each person will need two pieces of gridded paper (four pieces total) and a pencil.

1) Label the top horizontal line of two pieces of gridded paper with numbers and the left vertical line with letters of the alphabet. Tell your friend to do the same.

2) Take the first piece of gridded paper. Choose twenty squares at random where you will set your traps. Color in the squares you choose. Tell your friend to do the same. Keep it on your lap so you can look at it easily, but your friend can't. No peeking at each others' papers! Take out the other piece of gridded paper. You will use this paper to mark your guesses as you hunt for your friend's traps. It's fine if your friend can see this paper.

3) Begin the game by calling out a square by letter and number (like B5).

4) If your friend has a trap there, he or she must call out "Trap detected." If there is no trap there, your friend calls out "No traps." If you find a trap, mark that square with an "X" on your paper and repeat steps 3 and 4 until you get a "No traps" answer. Indicate a square with no traps with a circle or dot so you can keep track of what squares you've searched.

If the last square called was a "no traps," it is the other player's turn. The first player to find all the traps wins.

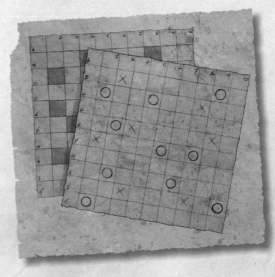

How to Draw a Map

Maps can prove quite valuable when monster hunting. A good map of the area can help you avoid pitfalls, lead you to a safer trail, and even show you the best place to spend the night, be it a convenient cave or a comfortable inn. If no map exists of the area, you can make one yourself. That way, you don't have to depend on your memories, and you can pass the map to the next wizard to travel that area.

Gridded paper is one of the best tools for making a map. Although terrain and even buildings and roads don't always follow straight lines, map makers can mark off lines through the grids to give a rough indication of what goes where. On the grid, one square should equal five feet of distance. If the map is just for you, making one as a general reminder is fine. But if other people may be using the map when you're not around, more detail and accuracy is a good idea. Future map readers will thank you for it.

Indicate creatures that you find in different areas. While they, of course, could move, it's helpful to know that a particular cave is home to kobolds, or vampires live in a specific house.

It's prudent to have multiple maps. One of the general area and more specific ones of complicated houses, castles, or cave systems. If you find you're squeezing too much information onto a map, that's a sure sign it's time to go to a more detailed layout.

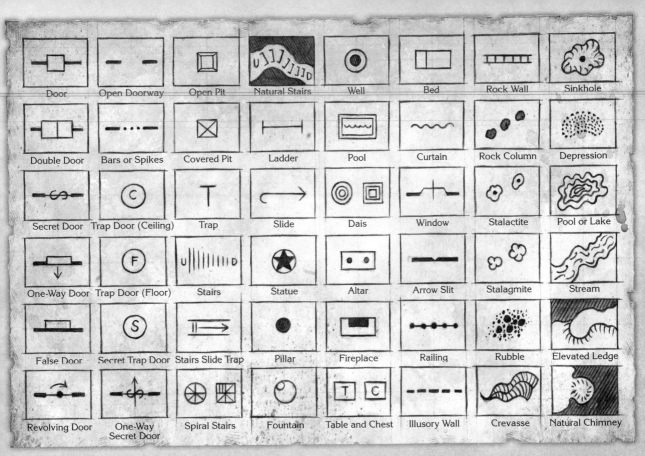

Door	Open Doorway	Open Pit	Natural Stairs	Well	Bed	Rock Wall	Sinkhole
Double Door	Bars or Spikes	Covered Pit	Ladder	Pool	Curtain	Rock Column	Depression
Secret Door	Trap Door (Ceiling)	Trap	Slide	Dais	Window	Stalactite	Pool or Lake
One-Way Door	Trap Door (Floor)	Stairs	Statue	Altar	Arrow Slit	Stalagmite	Stream
False Door	Secret Trap Door	Stairs Slide Trap	Pillar	Fireplace	Railing	Rubble	Elevated Ledge
Revolving Door	One-Way Secret Door	Spiral Stairs	Fountain	Table and Chest	Illusory Wall	Crevasse	Natural Chimney

The above drawing shows some standard map symbols. You can always make your own if what you need isn't present. Be sure to include a map key, which is a brief description of what each symbol means.

TIP!
PRACTICE YOUR MAP-MAKING SKILLS BY MAPPING YOUR HOME, SCHOOL, OR NEIGHBORHOOD. THE MORE MAPS YOU DRAW, THE FASTER YOU CAN DRAW THEM.

The above is a good example of a general area map.

How to Warn Other Wizards

When you're traveling, sometimes you'll need to leave signs for others following you. Perhaps you know that an area is frequented by a vampire every night, or you simply want someone to meet you at a certain location. Obviously you shouldn't carve detailed messages into trees or leave a note describing your every move tucked under a rock. This is a good occasion to use signs.

Signs can vary depending on where you travel. You can sketch them in sand or dirt, or create them with piled stones or twigs. The basic rules of signs are:

- Use only material available in the area.
- Do not damage the landscape in any way. You can use fallen twigs to create a sign, but never use twigs taken from trees.
- Signs should be easily removed by the last person to read them.

Other signals you may want to cultivate are light signals. You can either use your wand to produce a brief flash of light, or a mirror to reflect the sun, or light from your lantern covered with your hand. Basic signals are:

- One flash: "Camping here."
- Two flashes: "Meeting required."
- Three flashes: "Lost, please help!"[20]

Basic Trail Signs

This is the Trail

Right Turn

Left Turn

Warning

20 Threes usually mean help. If you remember only one basic signal, this is the one to remember!

Here are some examples of symbols you and your friends can establish beforehand. Keep the symbols simple but easily identifiable and, when possible, logical. For example, the ripple above for water is easily understood as it looks like waves. A crossed twig or lines for a buried item is a very old sign, "X marks the spot."

You may want to make signs easily understood to only you and your companions. Say you all hated a teacher at school who had a pet snake. A crude drawing of a snake or even an actual snakeskin could mean "Danger! Enemies close!" Secret signs you and your fellow hunters may want to develop are listed below. You can always leave a rolled-up parchment behind with these signs written in invisible ink (see page 22) if you want your signs to stay supersecret.

Monster feeding area	Good monster nearby; ask for help
Beware of humans	HIDE NOW!

HUNTING MONSTERS

If you're hunting monsters, you must understand them better than you understand your closest comrade.[21] On the following pages you'll find all the secrets to assist you in any monster encounter you might have.

[21] What good is it to use silver weapons against a medusa or garlic on a goblin?

When and Why to Hunt a Monster [22]

Long gone are the days when it was considered high style to wear clothing edged with griffon's mane or adorn a dining hall with a manticore's head. These days, monsters should only be killed if they pose a real threat.

There are three main reasons to hunt monsters:

Observation

Many wizardry schools keep a small menagerie on their grounds for study. All these monsters must be tracked, captured, and transported safely. This is extremely tricky, especially the task of transportation. If you are hunting monsters for observation, make sure you have containment and sleep spells memorized.

Evaluation

Often a monster will move into an area near a town or city. It could be a giant looking for a meal, or a group of goblins seeking a fight, or a sphinx just curious about the local theater. Until the monster makes its first move, though, no one knows what its intentions are. A townsperson may hire a wizard like you to track the monster and figure out what the monster wants.

Destruction

Unfortunately, there are occasions when a monster must be destroyed. This decision should never be made lightly and you should always have some companions with you when you attempt such an endeavor.

---

22 The first rule of monster hunting is "Know exactly what you're hunting and how it might hunt you!"

How to Trap a Zombie

While frightening, zombies pose little threat to the agile and intelligent wizard. Escape is simple: climb a tree or run away. Almost anyone can run faster than a zombie. However, the true monster hunter will not attempt escape without first studying the zombie.

A zombie does not rise unless compelled by dark magic and a wizard known as a necromancer must command its every move. By trapping the zombie, you can learn about the necromancer and foil the wizard's evil plans.

TIP!
ONLY ALLOW
ZOMBIES NEAR
THIS TRAP!

Tanglefoot Trap

Easy to build, this zombie trap will allow you to study the zombie in the field and release it before the evil wizard suspects its monster is missing.

Clear a small area of any sticks or branches. Set aside for later. Pour tanglefoot potion in a small puddle onto the ground. (See page 23.) You may need several batches. Stack branches around the potion and cover them with leaves. Be careful not to allow the leaves to stick to the potion.

Attract the zombie's attention. Limburger cheese helps. Lead the monster to the trap. Once the zombie has focused on chasing you, it has no choice but to follow. Jump over the trap. Unable to jump, the zombie will get stuck in the tanglefoot potion.

Study the zombie then leave the area. The tanglefoot potion will no longer be sticky after several hours and the zombie can escape.

Zombie Infiltration

Zombies notice speed, so if you can walk slow and lurch like a zombie, you should be able to walk with them for a short time unnoticed. I recommend practicing this with your friends.

Find three or more people to play. Choose one person to be the necromancer. Mark a start and finish line. Everyone but the necromancer lines up at the start. The necromancer waits at the finish line.

When the necromancer says "Zombies arise!" everyone starts walking as slowly as possible toward the finish line. Everyone must keep moving their feet forward at all times. Arms must be held out stiff and straight. If the necromancer sees someone stop, bend a knee or elbow, or lower his arms, the necromancer shouts the name of the person and "Back to the grave!" That person is then out of the game.

ZOMBIE TRAITS

Sight:
Usually humanoid; shambling walk; pale, rotting flesh.

Smell:
Your best sense when trying to detect a zombie. The more rank and rotted the smell, the longer the zombie has been reanimated and, therefore, the slower and clumsier it's apt to be.

Sound:
Shuffling sound as they walk, moaning voice.

How to Catch a Werewolf

You certainly wouldn't expect to have to trap a monster when you're resting for the night. However, what happens when you find your fellow monster hunter is really a werewolf?

Certain features can be clues. Long hair or long fingernails are usually traits of a werewolf, as are pointed teeth and yellow-tinged eyes. Your friend may become edgy as night approaches and the moon begins to rise. Once he or she begins to change, you must take action swiftly before the transformation to wolf is completed.

This is not as bad as it might sound. Changing from human to wolf is noisy and takes time, so you'll be able to create your trap.

Werewolf Trap

- Silver (powder works best, especially sparkly powder)
- White bread
- Sliced meat (werewolves prefer ham or turkey)
- Sliced cheese (Swiss or other pale cheese)
- Drinking glass with thin edges

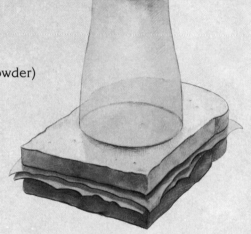

1) Use some (not all!) of the silver to create a partial circle about five feet in diameter. Conceal the circle with leaves or other items.

2) Make a sandwich from the meat, bread, and cheese. Use a glass to cut the sandwich into a circle.

3) Place the circular sandwich in the center of the silver powder circle.

4) Hide and wait for the werewolf.

5) When the werewolf arrives and takes the sandwich, complete the circle of silver so the werewolf is inside it.

6) The werewolf is trapped in the circle until the moon sets.

Why does circular food attract werewolves? Werewolves, especially those in the middle of their change, despise round things that remind them of the moon, the cause of their painful transformation. Put something circular and edible, preferably pale in color, in front of them and they will devour it as they wish to destroy the moon. If you have time, use an illusion spell to give it the appearance of the moon.

WEREWOLF TRAITS

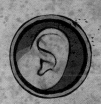

Sight:
When human—long hair, long fingernails, pointed teeth. When wolf—more intelligent eyes than a regular wolf, may have same color hair as person.

Smell:
Wet dog, faint when human, more pungent when wolf.

Sound:
Cracking sound when they first start the change.

How to Track a Vampire

If possible, never track a vampire at night. At night a vampire's powers are at their height and with its superior sense of hearing and smell, it can easily sense you on its trail.

As vampires are probably the most intelligent monsters around, aside from dragons, tracking them even during the day is very tricky. They can take four forms: human, bat, wolf, and mist. While tracking the form of bat or mist is near impossible, human and wolf is a bit easier. Look for tracks of human feet that suddenly change to wolf.[23]

Don dark clothing at night (if you absolutely MUST track them then) and colors that blend into the surroundings during the day. Leave all but the most essential items at home so you can be light on your feet and very quiet in your steps. Avoid conversation with your fellow hunters, and keep movement to a minimum.

The best place to find a vampire is its lair. Look for patterns in the tracks, places that the tracks often lead to or from. Even if the tracks seem to end in the middle of nowhere, chances are the vampire changed to mist or a bat and flew to a residence. As vampires have expensive tastes when it comes to homes, look for activity in a long-abandoned fine house or castle near your town, especially ones near graveyards. Watch it for a day or two. If you see no movement in or around the building during the day, but plenty at night, that is most likely the vampire's home.

---

[23] Differs from werewolf tracks, which show a lot of damage to the ground and surrounding area where the human tracks change to wolf. Vampire tracks will be human for one step and wolf the next.

Garlic is the best defense against a vampire. They find the smell extremely offensive. (Think of the most horrible stench you've ever encountered and increase it a hundredfold!) Wearing cloves of garlic on a string about one's neck works well, but eating food seasoned with garlic is believed to be better protection. While the smell of a garlic string would discourage a vampire from trying to bite you, if you've eaten the garlic, then the smell and taste is in your blood. That way, a vampire will have no interest in you as a possible meal.

You may also repel a vampire by sprinkling powdered garlic in water. Rigging a bucket trap to dump garlic water over a vampire is a popular method. Some people fill animal bladders to create garlic water-filled missiles. Some are calling these items garlic "balloons."

Practice hunting vampires with friends and balloons in warm weather. It's a fun way to stay in shape for vampire hunting, as well as to cool off when it's hot outside!

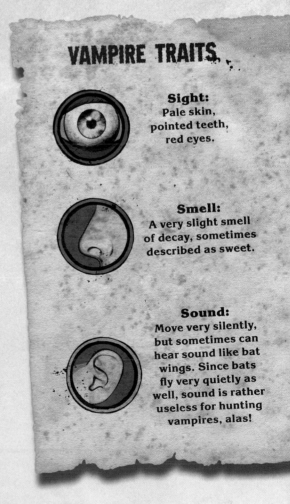

VAMPIRE TRAITS

Sight:
Pale skin, pointed teeth, red eyes.

Smell:
A very slight smell of decay, sometimes described as sweet.

Sound:
Move very silently, but sometimes can hear sound like bat wings. Since bats fly very quietly as well, sound is rather useless for hunting vampires, alas!

Vampire Repellent

Throw vampire-repelling stakes to fend off any attacking vampires. To make the stakes, toast a bread slice. Spread butter or olive oil on the toast. Sprinkle toast with dried garlic and, if you like, parmesan cheese and oregano. Cut into long strips to resemble stakes.

If you hit the vampire with the stake, the toast sticks to the vampire and irritates their skin. If you just manage to throw the stake near the vampire, they will be so repelled by the smell that they will retreat.

TIP!
THESE STAKES CAN ALSO BE A TASTY TREAT BEFORE VAMPIRE HUNTING!

How to Fight a Medusa

A medusa can turn her enemies to stone with just a simple glance. In many storybooks, the brave hero defeats the medusa with nothing but a mirror, reflecting her gaze and forcing her to turn herself into stone.

However, do not, under any circumstances, fight a medusa with your mother's beauty mirror! For starters, a medusa is unlikely to be the first creature you encounter upon your adventure. That means your mirror will be subjected to all the jostling of travel, whether you go by wagon or dragon. Imagine how silly you'll feel when you pull out your mirror to show a medusa, only to find it broken. Silly is the last thing you'll feel. Or perhaps you'll feel silly for an eternity, no one knows!

MEDUSA TRAITS

Sight:
Humanoid, snakes for hair, sometimes scaly skin

Smell:
Ocean water, fish

Sound:
Hissing. Medusas seem incapable of quieting the snakes in their hair. How they ever get to sleep at night, no one knows!

Mirror Shield

You can use thin metal[24] to make a medusa-repelling shield by making a lightweight frame and stretching the thin metal over it.

- One piece of cardboard at least two feet square
- Thin metal
- Masking tape
- Pipe cleaners

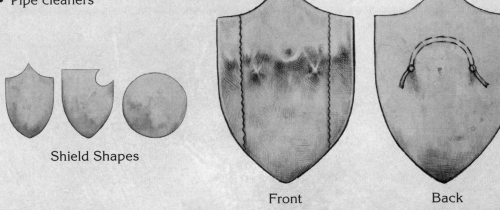

Shield Shapes

Front

Back

1) Using one of the shapes above as a guide, cut a shield out of the cardboard.

2) Poke two holes in the middle of the shield about three inches apart.

3) Knot one end of a pipe cleaner and pull it through one of the holes.

4) Pull the other end of the pipe cleaner through the second hole and then knot the pipe cleaner on the same side as the other knot. This will be the handle for the shield. Cover both knots with tape.

5) Spread thin metal over the cardboard on the side with the pipe cleaner knots.

6) Fold edges of thin metal over edges of cardboard. Use glue to hold in place if needed.

7) Spread thin metal as smooth as possible. The smoother it is, the better the reflection and the better your shield will work.

You are now ready to face a medusa. Once she is turned to stone, you have a day to transport her to a secure location if you so desire.

---

24 The great weapons wizard Alum Foil has invented thin sheets of metal, so thin that you can fold them like paper! This thin metal is available in wizarding supply shops and anywhere food is sold.

How to Banish a Ghost

Ghosts can appear anywhere—in an ancient castle or in your own living room. Many ghosts can cause damage to your hearing or even your mind with their wailing. As soon as a ghost appears, stuff wax plugs or cotton balls in your ears to muffle the sound.

Don't bother trying to fight a ghost. Instead, get it talking. A ghost usually appears for a reason. You must determine what it needs and help it so that it can rest once its mission on this plane is complete.

After you've learned some details about the ghost, find a safe place to think and plan. To keep the ghost from following you, you will need some salt. Ghosts hate salt. Sprinkle some salt across the doorway of a room to prevent the ghost from entering it. Then stay in that room to plan how to help the ghost. You need time to think and make notes and you can't do that if the ghost is screeching in your ear.

GHOST TRAITS

Sight:
Varies from invisible to almost solid. Usually takes similar form to what they were in life.

Smell:
Sometimes none, sometimes a scent associated with the ghost's former life. For example, the ghost of a baker may smell like fresh bread.

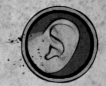

Sound:
Wailing. Block your ears as soon as you hear them to prevent any damage.

Ghost Puzzle

Here's a mystery involving not just one ghost, but four: Baran, Alrac, Pryral, and Gorat. To help them rest, you must determine what they were in life, how they died, and why they were still on this earthly plane. The clues are:

- Two ghost names begin with the same letter as their role in life.
- Gorat was always hungry, but now he's very thin.
- Alrac liked alchemy; Baran liked bludgeoning.
- Royal rivalries and revenge last beyond death.
- The person killed by a potion accident wants the right formula published.

Using the grid below, you can solve the mystery of the ghosts. The marks for the first clue are already made.

GHOST PUZZLE		Role in Life				What They Want			
✗ = Not possible ✓ = Answer		Princess	Wizard	Warrior	Goblin	Family Paid	Revenge	Lunch	Potion Formula
Name	Baran								
	Alrac								
	Pryral	✓	✗	✗	✗				
	Gorat	✗	✗	✗	✓				
How They Died	Fighting Dragon								
	Potion Accident								
	Killed by Rival								
	Crushed by Boulder								
What They Want	Family Paid								
	Revenge								
	Lunch								
	Potion Formula								

How to Distract a Goblin

Sometimes known as the mosquitoes of the monster world, goblins may seem more silly than threatening. Do not underestimate them! Many monster hunters have lost their lives to a goblin because they were laughing too hard.

As goblin behavior is well-known and the field of goblin studies is thoroughly saturated, the only reason for trapping a goblin is to get specific information from it. Goblins often attack in a group. Trying to kill them all will probably pose more danger to you than them. Besides, you don't want to waste all your magic on them, especially if they attack in the early morning and you have a long day of monster hunting ahead of you. It's better to distract them.

Goblins are greedy. They will stop in their tracks to pick up anything of value. Throw something at them that appears to be a bag of coins and they will fight among themselves over who can get to the bag first while you make your escape.

GOBLIN TRAITS

Sight:
About three feet tall, yellow, green, or red skin, flattened face

Smell:
Spoiled milk

Sound:
Snorting and snuffling.

Goblin Coin Toss

Train for distracting goblins before you head out on your adventure using this game. You can practice either on your own or make a game with friends.

- Large box (with sides at least two feet square)
- At least ten old socks
- Small coins (not too valuable!) or buttons for practice (does not work for real goblins!)
- String

Step 1

Steps 2–3

Steps 4–5

Step 6

1) Cut the box so it is six inches deep and at least two feet wide and high.

2) Cut holes about three inches in diameter in the box. You can either space them in a pattern or irregularly.

3) Draw goblin heads around each hole.

4) Fill the toe of each sock with ten to fifteen coins of small value.

5) Tie top of sock closed with string.[25]

6) Set box on the ground and stand ten feet away. Try to toss the bags through the holes. The better your aim is, the better prepared you'll be to throw things at goblins. As you get better, increase the distance so you won't have to get too close to the goblins when you meet them on your quest.

---

[25] Check to see if the sock will fit through the holes before making more.

How to Hunt a Kraken

Krakens are the most common underwater monsters. Large and capable of moving swiftly through water, these amazing and terrifying monsters are the dragons of the sea. You can tell when one is nearby from the water turbulence and absence of fish.

Nets (see instructions on page 16–17), can be used to capture krakens. Simply enchant them to be the appropriate size. Set a net across rocks or a coral reef and bait it by asking a dolphin or seal to wait on the other side. When the kraken sees its prey, it will charge, so intent on killing that it will not see the net.

Once captured, find a boat and tow the kraken to a desired location, either far, far away from civilization or to an underwater zoo.

KRAKEN TRAITS

Sight:
Monstrous squid, long, thin

Smell:
Rotted fish, seawater.

Sound:
Makes a cry like an angry whale

Enchanted Vessel

As boats are not always easy to find, making a temporary enchanted vessel is a surefire way to get the underwater monster where it needs to go. Once your boat is complete, you can enchant it to be large enough to hold you and five other people or even tow a sea monster. It will accept verbal commands, so no knowledge of sailing is necessary!

- One rectangular (8½ x 11 inches) sheet of wax-coated paper or thin metal (see page 55)

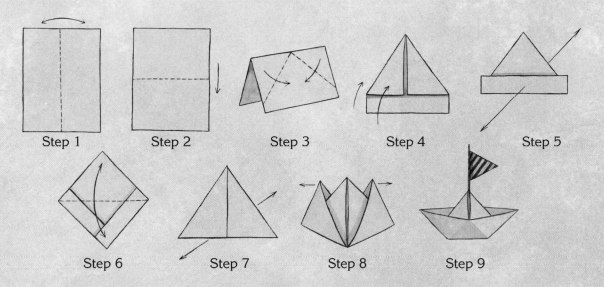

Step 1   Step 2   Step 3   Step 4   Step 5

Step 6   Step 7   Step 8   Step 9

1) With long side of paper vertical (like a portrait), fold in half lengthwise, then unfold it.

2) Fold in half downward.

3) Fold top corners toward center fold.

4) Fold bottom edges up. Fold on both front and back.

5) Pull bottom edges of center fold outward until you get a flat square.

6) Fold up front and back layers to form a triangle.

7) Pull bottom center edges until you get a flat square.

8) Hook your fingers under the top layer of paper and pull outward to form a boat shape. Flatten the bottom edge.

9) Open center edges slightly to form the finished boat. If you plan to sail your vessel, stick a toothpick with a paper flag through the center.

How to Evade a Griffon

The most important thing to remember when escaping from a griffon is do not run! You will never outrun a griffon and it makes them angrier and more determined to catch you. Look for cover: a tree, rocks, water. Once you're hidden, then you can dig in your monster-hunting pack and find the item that will save you—your double doll.

Once you have your double doll in hand, throw it into the open and cast an illusion spell so it looks like you. The griffon will snatch up the doll and take it home for dinner. The griffon won't look closely at your doll until it returns to its nest, thus giving you plenty of time to move to a safer location.

GRIFFON TRAITS

Sight:
Eagle's head, lion's body, wings, and claws.

Smell:
Fresh meat

Sound:
Cawing, flapping of wings

Double Doll

Remember to make this doll before heading out to monster hunt! You won't have time to craft it on the spot if a griffon spies you from the air.

- Ball of yarn or string, any color (a color close to your skin or hair color, or your favorite color aids the illusion)
- Piece of cardboard about 8½ x11 inches
- Scissors

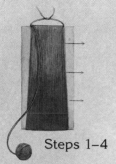

Steps 1–4

Steps 5–6

Steps 7–11

1) Wrap yarn two hundred times around long side of cardboard forming a bundle.

2) Cut seven pieces of yarn six inches long.

3) Thread one piece of yarn between bundle and the top of the cardboard and tie tightly.

4) Slide bundle off cardboard.

5) Tie another piece of yarn around bundle about two inches from first yarn. This forms the head of your double.

6) Split bundle under the head into three sections. Middle section should be about one hundred strands and the two side sections should be about fifty strands.

7) Tie a piece of yarn around middle section about three inches from second string. This forms the double's middle.

8) Tie one piece of yarn around each of the side sections, about three inches from second string. This forms the arms, which should be proportional to the head and body.

9) Divide the middle section in half.

10) Tie one piece of yarn around each half of the middle section, near the end of the yarn. This will form the legs.

11) Cut off the excess strings from the arms and legs one half inch from the ties.[26]

12) Dress or decorate your doll to resemble you.[27]

---

[26] If the arms and legs seem too long or too short, readjust the ties before cutting.

[27] You can use an illusion spell, of course, but it takes less magic to transform the doll when it already looks like you.

How to Disgust an Ogre

So you've been captured by an ogre who wants to eat you. That wasn't very smart, was it? Now you're sitting on a shelf in the ogre's pantry and you can hear him rattling pots and lighting a fire in the stove. It's suppertime, and you're on the menu! What to do?

While ogres are much bigger and uglier (usually) than humans, we do share an aversion to eating spoiled food. You certainly wouldn't eat a rotten apple or moldy cheese! So think about what makes you not want to eat your food and make yourself look as rotten and disgusting as possible. You have an advantage over a piece of moldy fruit, because you can act sick as well as look sick.

I recommend crying, fake vomiting, and complaining of stomach pains as much as you can. If you can find some red juice, use it to draw dots on your body so you look like you have plague or a rash. Even if this doesn't completely kill the ogre's appetite, it will likely look for something else in their pantry before deciding to eat you, thus giving you a chance to escape.

OGRE TRAITS

Sight:
Large, ugly, heavy.

Smell:
Extreme body odor

Sound:
Grunts, incapable of walking quietly

Dirt Cake Recipe[28]

Legend tells of a famous baker once captured by an ogre. The ogre demanded that this baker bake him a cake. Upon its completion, the ogre planned to plop the baker into the cake and eat him too! The baker thought long and hard and came up with a plan. The baker made the following dessert, told the ogre it was made of dirt, and the ogre was so disgusted that it instantly fell ill, allowing the baker to escape.

- One large (16 oz.) package of hard chocolate cookies
- Two four-serving size packages of instant chocolate pudding
- 3½ cups milk
- 12 oz. whipped topping
- Candy worms
- Mixing bowl
- Rolling pin
- Bag
- Clear glass dish or eight glasses (for single-servings)

1) Mix instant pudding and milk in bowl. Let stand for five minutes.

2) While you're waiting, place cookies in a sealed bag and crush with a rolling pin.

3) Add the whipped topping to the pudding mixture.

4) Add about half of the crushed cookies to the mixture.

5) Put a layer of the mixture in the glass dish or the glasses, followed by cookie crumbs. Repeat until filled, making last layer cookie crumbs.

6) Chill overnight.

7) For maximum gross-out, add the candy worms on top.

---

28 This recipe comes from a far-off land, so many of these ingredients may be exotic and hard to find.

How to Blind a Beholder

Beholders are nasty critters with many eyes. Each eye has a different and terrifying power, from the ability to petrify an enemy, to the ability to render any spell useless. It is nearly impossible to hide from or surprise a beholder. Trickery is your best option for this beast.

Tie some daisies or other flowers to your monster catcher (page 16). The flowers confuse the beholder because they look like eyes. Climb above the monster's lair or other area the beholder is known

to frequent. Then have a fellow monster hunter or a magical double of yourself (see page 63) lure the beholder into position. When the beholder is below you, drop the net covering the beholder's head, body and, most importantly, eyes.

The beholder will become briefly disoriented and will be incapable of casting any of its powerful spells on you. A simple blindness or sleep spell will keep it contained until you can move it to a safe location.

TIP!
IF YOU DON'T HAVE TIME TO MODIFY YOUR NET, PULL OUT ONE OF THE BLANKETS FROM YOUR BEDROLL.

BEHOLDER TRAITS

Sight:
Shaped like a ball with no legs; many eyes on tentacle-like stalks.

Smell:
As they cannot brush their teeth, very bad breath that can be smelled at a distance.

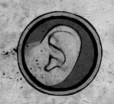

Sound:
Faint hissing and whipping of tentacles.

Blind Beholder's Bluff

Get out your monster catcher (see page 16). Then choose one person to be the beholder. That person cannot move their feet, although they can lean and reach with their arms.

Everyone surrounds the beholder and tries to throw the monster catcher over its head. If the beholder touches someone who does not have the monster catcher, the person is out of the game. If the beholder touches someone who does have the monster catcher, the person has to throw it immediately to someone else or that person is out.

When the monster catcher is over the beholder, the person who threw it shouts "Beholder's blinded!" and the game is over. The person who blinded the beholder can be the beholder next time.

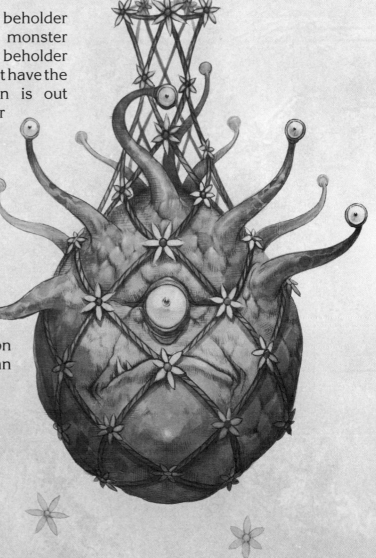

TIP!
IF YOU DON'T WANT TO PLAY WITH YOUR MONSTER CATCHER, YOU CAN USE A SCARF INSTEAD.

How to Fool a Sphinx

If a dragon threatens your town, call a warrior. If a sphinx threatens your town, call a wizard. Wizards are taught how to think when they study magic, so you have a very valuable tool when confronting a sphinx.

While threatening, sphinxes often can be defeated through mind-power alone, a true rarity in the monster world! Usually, a sphinx will ask you a riddle. If you solve it, you then get to pose a riddle to the sphinx. If the sphinx cannot guess the answer to your riddle, it will be compelled to honor your wishes.[29]

Be creative when confronted with a riddle. A very famous sphinx once asked this riddle: "What goes on four legs in the morning, two in the afternoon, and three in the evening?" The correct answer is a human. A human crawls when an infant, walks on two legs during the middle of its life, and in old age, a human walks with two legs and a cane. The trick to this riddle is that "morning, afternoon, and night" are not times of day after all, but rather refer to the lifespan of a human.

SPHINX TRAITS

Sight:
Winged lion

Smell:
Cigar smoke

Sound:
Usually pretty quiet

---

[29] Many a sphinx, however, was so overcome with grief over being out-riddled by a mere human that they threw themselves off a cliff rather than live with the knowledge of their defeat.

Here are some other riddles a sphinx might try. See if you can figure out the right answer:

- What has green hair, wrinkled skin, and wears lots of rings?

- The colder it is, the denser I be. The warmer I get, I begin to fly free.

- I speak nothing and say much.

Riddle Writing

Now that you have the general idea how to solve riddles, try writing a few of your own.

First, choose an object for the riddle's answer. For our example, we'll use a gold coin. To come up with a hint, think about the object. How is it made or how does it grow? Gold coins must be forged in a fire, so our first hint could be "Born of fire."

Next, think about what the object is. Coins are often associated with greedy people or people who desperately want treasure. As riddles are always improved with rhyme, the second clue could be "Symbol of desire."

Then, describe how the object looks, but do not be too obvious. Giving an object a human characteristic makes the riddle a bit trickier. Gold glitters in the sun, so our third clue could be "Winking in sunlight."

Lastly, consider what the object does or causes. For a fourth clue, "I cause many a fight" could work, as the desire for riches often brings out the worst in people.

So, our riddle is:

Born of fire,
Symbol of desire,
Winking in sunlight,
I cause many a fight.

Answer: Gold coin

Creating Riddles with Objects

Here are some other objects you could use to create riddles. Try using one of these to write a riddle of your own that could fool a sphinx!

- Rock
- Feather
- Glass
- Horse
- Ink
- Flower
- Milk
- Glass
- Honey
- Dog
- Boat
- Egg

How to Entertain a Monster

Should you be captured by a monster in the midst of a monster hunt, remember you're already ahead of the game. The monster captured you because it found you interesting. Your life now depends on remaining interesting until you are rescued or can escape.

Usually, a monster captures a wizard because it's curious or bored. When you're in the monster's lair, look around, and see what the monster likes. If you see lots of books, tell it amusing stories. If you see treasure, compliment it on its wealth and, if the monster seems chatty, ask it to tell you stories about how it found the treasure (even if the story is rather gory, try to look engrossed rather than scared).

Monsters that capture humans usually love games. Many live solitary lives, so having someone to play with is a novelty. Longer games like chess are ideal, but even a simple game of Draw Claws (so named for monsters playing this game in the sand by drawing lines with their talons) can go on for a very long time, until the monster falls asleep and you can make your escape.

Draw Claws Game

1) Find a friend to practice the Draw Claws game with you, so you will be prepared to play it for hours if the need ever arises! To begin, make a grid[30] of dots in the ground with a stick or on paper with a pen.

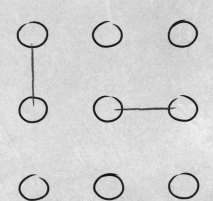

2) Choose someone to draw first. (I advise picking the monster!) The first player puts a line between two dots. The next player then puts a line between two dots.

3) Continue back and forth in this manner. Each player's goal is to complete as many squares as possible. When a person completes a square, they put their initial in it, indicating that is now their territory. My initial is A, so I'll put that in the square. If a player completes a square, they get an extra turn, so I'll add another line. You can block the other player by adding lines to their squares.

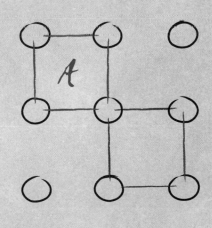

4) Once the board is filled, the person with the most squares wins the game.

TIP!
TRY TO ANTICIPATE YOUR OPPONENT'S MOVES AND PLAN YOUR MOVES ACCORDINGLY!

---

30 The example uses a simple 3 x 3 grid, but you can make it as large as you like. By making a VERY big grid, you can have a game that can last for days!

How to Recruit a Monster

Every once in a while, you may need to recruit one monster to help you hunt another. While approaching a monster may sound like a daunting task, it is possible to convince monsters to help you. These requests usually work best with more intelligent monsters, such as vampires, medusas, or werewolves (in their non-wolf state, of course). Even less intelligent monsters such as ogres or goblins can be recruited. Some people even prefer monsters that aren't known for their intelligence because there is less chance of them turning on you.

Selecting the right recruit requires knowing the habits of the monster. Different tactics work on different monsters. It's especially good to know how the monster feels about other monsters. Beholders detest medusas because, since beholders have so many eyes, medusas are especially dangerous. Vampires have a great disdain for werewolves because they compete over territory or animal blood.

The secret to convincing the monster to join your party comes down to a most simple kind of magic. Most monsters adore music, but few monsters cultivate the art of performing. Playing a lovely tune just before you approach a monster can encourage it to become your companion before you even open your mouth to ask.

Pan Pipes

Often associated with satyrs, the pan pipes are a very melodious and soothing musical instrument. You can make them yourself out of bamboo, paper tubes, or straws. Just be sure to practice before you use it on a monster!

- Twelve hollow pipes or straws (between ¼ to 1 inch in diameter; large drinking straws work very well)
- Cardboard
- Clear double-sided adhesive strips[31]
- Modeling clay

1) Cut two straws each, of the following lengths:
   6 inches
   5¾ inches
   5¼ inches
   4¾ inches
   4 inches
   3½ inches

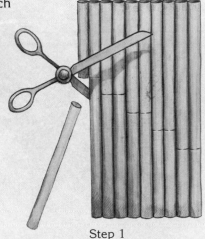

Step 1

2) Cut two cardboard strips six inches long by three inches wide.

3) Lay a piece of double-sided adhesive on one side of each cardboard strip.

4) Place the straws on the adhesive strip in pairs. Start with the two longest on the far right, placing them right next to each other. Lay the other pairs separating each slightly (about the width of one straw).

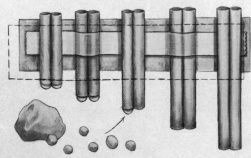

Steps 2–6

5) Place the straws between the two pieces of cardboard. Press together slightly to make sure the adhesive sticks. You can trim the cardboard if it extends too long.

6) Roll clay into small balls and use to plug the bottom end of each straw.

7) Test your pipes by blowing over the open end. You can adjust the tone by adding or removing clay from the end.

8) Decorate your pipes by drawing designs on the cardboard.

---

31 Known in some lands as "double-sided tape."

How to Outwit Almost Any Monster

Thousands of different monsters inhabit the lands around us, too many to describe in one small book. We have covered the most common and most dangerous of monsters with specific advice, and with more monsters listed at the back of this book for your reference. In the case that you track, encounter, fight, or trap a monster not detailed in this book, rest assured you can still have a safe and successful adventure. Just follow these basic tips.

Track

When you're tracking a monster, your sense of sight is your best tool. Look carefully at the ground for footprints. Also keep an eye out for broken branches, piles of droppings, or other signs that a monster recently used the area as either a hunting ground or a sleeping spot. Try to not only identify the kind of monster, but also how many there are.

Encounter

Once you encounter a monster, running is absolutely the worst and most foolish thing you can do. Almost all monsters are faster than a human and running attracts many of them, especially flying creatures. Instead remain still and quiet until you deduce the monster's intention.

Avoid direct eye contact. At best, a monster views it as a challenge. At worst, the monster can hypnotize you or turn you to stone! Watch the monster's hands (if humanoid) or mouth and claws (if more animal-like) instead of the monster's eyes.

Fight

There is a reason why wizards are called "wizards" and not "fighters." Rely on defensive spells and ranged weapon spells. Don't go running up to a monster swinging a sword. Look for trees you can climb, and rocks that you can hide behind. Both those locations are good for casting spells.

Trap

A monster catcher works extremely well, especially when combined with a sleep or daze spell. The danger of trapping is usually not actually ensnaring the creature, but rather what to do after you've caught the monster. Far too many wizards have been killed as they contemplated what to do with the monster they had caught.

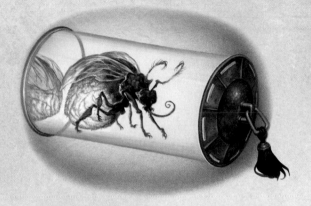

Once you've trapped a monster, begin transportation immediately. If for some reason you cannot cast a teleportation spell, physically transport the monster as quickly as possible. Use sleep or stunning spells to keep it under control. Levitation spells eliminate the need to carry the monster. Transporting the monster to locations more than a day's walk away is not recommended.

Above all, never underestimate a monster's intelligence (especially for vampires, sphinxes, and dragons). If they appear to be acting stupid, chances are it's a trick.

Basic Monster Hunting Rules

1) Know what you're hunting.

2) Know why you're hunting it.

3) Know what you'll do with the monster once the hunt is complete.

MORE MONSTERS

Scale of Hostility

①	②	③	④	⑤
Friendly	Indifferent	Cranky	Mean	Run for Cover!

Scale of Intelligence

❶	❷	❸	❹	❺
Idiot	Stupid	Average	Smart	Brilliant

Name	Sight	Smell	Sound	Location	Hostility	Intelligence	Best Tactic
Basilisk	Large gray reptile, spines across back	Wet stone, rotted meat	Shuffling sound, dragging tail	Wilderness area, warm climates	④	❶	Avoid if possible; if you must confront, use medusa tactics
Bugbear	Large goblin, bearlike nose	Bad body odor	Grunting, clinking of chains they use for armor	Mountains, caves	④	❸	Do not engage unless you have odds on your side
Chimera	Three heads: dragon, lion, and goat	Rotten meat and goat dung	Growling and bleating	Caves, various climates	⑤	❷	Flying creature—use griffon tactics
Chromatic Dragon	Large, majestic, scaled creature with wings	Varies by color	Growling of head and of stomach	Caves, various climates (depending on dragon)	⑤	❺	DO NOT ENGAGE! Experienced monster hunters only!
Cyclops	Giant, one eye	Poor vision, tend to step in monster poop	Very loud footsteps	Various climates and areas	④	❸	If captured, use ogre tactics
Displacer Beast	Catlike, six legs	Smell of ozone	Snarling, faint humming	Forests, caves	⑤	❷	Treat this beast as you would a creature with illusion abilities

Name	Sight	Smell	Sound	Location	Hostility	Intelligence	Best Tactic
Doppelganger	Can mimic any humanoid it wishes	Smell part of illusion	Sound part of illusion	Anywhere!	4	4	Ask questions that only the true person can answer
Dryad	Like tree in humanoid form	Wood, fall leaves	Wood creaking, even when humanoid	Forests	3	3	Normally doesn't attack unless threatened
Gargoyle	Stone statue	Wet stone	Creaking sound when moving	Castle, other man-made places, caves, cliffs	3	2	Flying beast, use griffon tactics
Giant	Um . . . it's giant?	Depends on giant and its personal hygiene habits	Thump when walk	Wide open spaces	1	3	Standard combat, but only if provoked
Hag	Can appear as ugly woman or beautiful lady	Spoiled stew, cats	Speaks like human	Forests, swamps, wild areas	5	4	Very intelligent magic-user; use best spells
Harpy	Winged woman with claws	Rotten eggs	Screeching, fluttering of wings	Swamps, coasts, caves	3	4	Use griffon tactics
Hobgoblin	Large goblin	Burned dinner	Guttural speech, clanking of armor	Warm hills and mountains	4	2	Smarter and stronger than goblins, standard combat
Hydra	Reptile with many heads	Old pond water	Hissing, splashing	Swamps, bogs, caverns	5	1	Can only be destroyed if all the heads are severed
Kobold	Small dragonlike humanoids	Mold	Grunting, click of nails on stone	Usually near dragon lairs, dark places	4	2	Can fight, but usually cowardly, especially when it is solitary
Lich	Part skeleton, part ghost	Ancient dust	Hollow voice, creaking joints	Ancient cities, castles, temples	4	5	Can damage with a touch, stay out of arm's reach
Manticore	Lion body, human face, dragon wings	Rotten meat	Growls, dragon wings flapping	Caves, mountains	5	2	Not very intelligent or agile, but fight carefully

Name	Sight	Smell	Sound	Location	Hostility	Intelligence	Best Tactic
Metallic Dragon	Majestic, sparkles	Varies according to color	Growling, roaring	Varies according to color	1 2	5	Be polite, most will help you if you're on the side of good
Minotaur	Bull-like humanoid	Blood	Snorts, grunts like a bull's	Caves, likes mazes	4	3	Approach carefully, may help you escape a maze
Mummy	Humanoid wrapped in bandages	Ancient dust	Moans, grunts, shuffling footsteps	Ancient tombs, castles	3	1	Use zombie tactics
Naga	Large snake with human face	Old pennies	Faint hissing, slithering	Caves, temples	5	4	Since it slithers, if you climb you can get away, may be friendly at times
Nightmare	Large black horse	Burned horsehair	Neighing, hoofbeats	Anywhere with flat land	4	2	Normally you need to worry more about who's riding it!
Nymph	Short woman's build, graceful	Soap bubbles	Very musical voice, likes singing	Forest	2	3	Dislikes humans, but if you respect the land around you, might win its trust
Owlbear	Body of bear, head of owl	A bear after a winter's hibernation	Grunts, hoots	Forest, cave	3	1	Usually functions as a guard
Phoenix	Birdlike, covered in flames	Campfire	A very sweet birdsong	Deserts, arid climate	1	3	Normally shy, can befriend with sweet fruits
Rakshasa	Humanoid with head of a large cat	Jasmine	Treads softly, growls, purrs	Loves palaces and fancy places	3	4	Not inclined to fight humans on sight unless there's a war going on

Name	Sight	Smell	Sound	Location	Hostility	Intelligence	Best Tactic
Roc	Large bird	Whatever it killed last	Large wing flaps, caws	Mountains	2	1	Usually leaves humans alone unless threatened, use griffon tactics
Skeleton	Bones only	Faint rot	Clattering of bones	Caves, dungeons, tombs	4	1	Use zombie tactics
Treant	A large tree with a face	Autumn leaves	Perfectly quiet when still, loud when walking	Forests	2	3	Friendly to humans unless they are hostile to forest
Troll	Humanoid, hulking, green skin	Rotten eggs	Thumping, grunting	Anywhere	3	2	Use giant tactics
Wyvern	Dragonlike	Spoiled meat	Growling	Caves, cliffs	4	1	Not as smart as a dragon— use griffon tactics

PREPARE FOR ADVENTURE

Discover the world of D&D® and explore the realms of fantasy fiction—with Wizards of the Coast's Books for Young Readers. By equipping yourself with the *New York Times* best-selling Practical Guide series and our other D&D-inspired titles, you can get ready for adventures of your own.

FIND THEM ALL AT YOUR FAVORITE BOOKSELLER.

 DUNGEONSANDDRAGONS.COM

DUNGEONS & DRAGONS

NEVER SPLIT THE PARTY